Back to my home I dare not go.
For if I do my mother will say,

"Did you ever see a bear
combing his hair
down by the bay?"

4

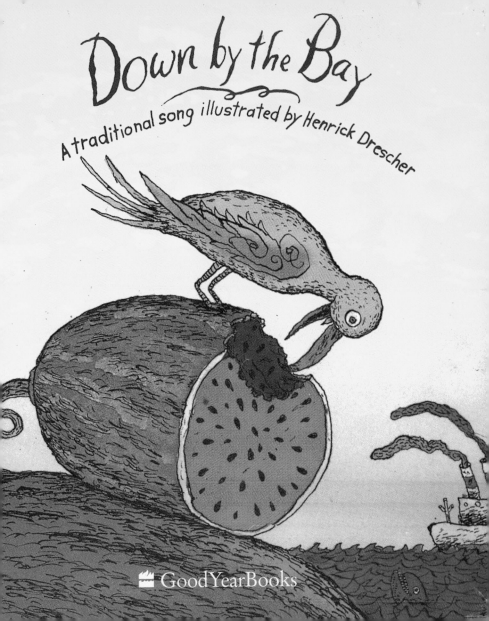

Down by the Bay

A traditional song illustrated by Henrick Drescher

GoodYearBooks

Down by the bay, where the watermelons grow,

"Did you ever see a bee
with a sun-burned knee
down by the bay?"

"Did you ever see a moose
    kissing a goose
    down by the bay?"

"Did you ever see a whale
with a polka dot tail
down by the bay?"

"Did you ever see a fish
sailing in a dish
down by the bay?"

"Did you ever see a cat
in a tall black hat
down by the bay?"

What could you see
sitting in a tree
down by the bay?